Chicken Licken

illustrated by Elisabeth Moseng

One day, a nut fell
on Chicken Licken.

"Ouch! The sky is
falling down!" said
Chicken Licken.
"I must tell the King."

On the way, he met
Henny Penny.

"The sky is falling down,"
said Chicken Licken.
"I'm going to tell
the King."

"I'll come too,"
said Henny Penny.

And off they went
to find the King.

On the way, they met
Cocky Locky.

"The sky is falling down,"
said Chicken Licken.
"I'm going to tell
the King."

11

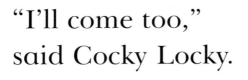

"I'll come too,"
said Cocky Locky.

And off they went
to find the King.

12

TO THE CASTLE

13

On the way, they met
Ducky Lucky.

"The sky is falling down,"
said Chicken Licken.
"I'm going to tell
the King."

15

"I'll come too,"
said Ducky Lucky.

And off they went
to find the King.

16

On the way, they met
Drakey Lakey.

"The sky is falling down,"
said Chicken Licken.
"I'm going to tell
the King."

"I'll come too,"
said Drakey Lakey.

And off they went
to find the King.

On the way, they met
Goosey Loosey.

"The sky is falling down,"
said Chicken Licken.
"I'm going to tell
the King."

"I'll come too," said
Goosey Loosey.

And off they went
to find the King.

23

On the way, they met
Foxy Loxy.

"The sky is falling down,"
they said. "We're going
to tell the King."

"The King lives here,"
said Foxy Loxy.
"Follow me."

TO THE CASTLE

25

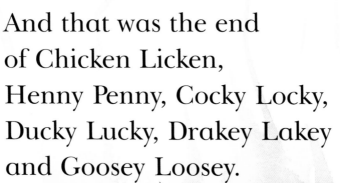

And that was the end
of Chicken Licken,
Henny Penny, Cocky Locky,
Ducky Lucky, Drakey Lakey
and Goosey Loosey.

Read It Yourself is a series of graded readers designed to give young children a confident and successful start to reading.

Level 2 is for children who are familiar with some simple words and can read short sentences. Each story in this level contains frequently repeated phrases which help children to read more fluently. Every page in the story is accompanied by a detailed illustration of the main action, which aids understanding of the text and encourages interest and enjoyment.

About this book

The story is told in a way which uses regular repetition of the main words and phrases. This enables children to recognise the words more and more easily as they progress through the book. An adult can help them to do this by pointing at the first letter of each word, and sometimes making the sound that the letter makes. Children will probably need less help as the story progresses.

Beginner readers need plenty of help and encouragement.